MONSTER By Mistake!

Fossel Remains

Adapted by **Paul Kropp**

Based on the screenplay by
Deborah Jarvis

Graphics by **Studio 345**

WINDING
STAIR
PRESS

Monster By Mistake
Theme Song

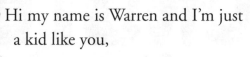

Hi my name is Warren and I'm just
a kid like you,

Or I was until I found evil
Gorgool's magic Jewel.

Then he tricked me and I read
a spell, now every
time I sneeze,

Monster By
Mistake . .

My sister Tracy tries the
Spell Book.

She never gets it right.

But Tracy doesn't ever give
up, 'cause you know one day
she might

Find the words that will
return me to my former width
and height.

I'm a Monster By Mista . . . . ah . . . . ah . . .

I'm gonna tell you 'bout Johnny the
    Ghost,

He's a wisecracking,
    trumpet playing
    friend.

He lives up in the
attic (shhh . . . Mom and
Dad don't know)

Johnny always has
    a helping hand
    to lend.

My secret Monster-iffic life always keeps
    me on the run.

And I have a funny
    feeling that the
    story's just begun.

Everybody thinks it's
    pretty awesome
    I've become

A Monster By Mistake!

I'm a Monster By Mistake!

I'm a Monster By Mistake!

Monster by Mistake
Text © 2002 by Winding Stair
Graphics © 2002 by Monster by Mistake Enterprises Ltd.
Monster By Mistake Created by Mark Mayerson
Produced by CCI Entertainment Ltd. and Catapult Productions
Series Executive Producers: Arnie Zipursky and Kim Davidson

National Library of Canada Cataloging in Publication Data

Kropp, Paul, 1948-
  Fossel Remains

(Monster by mistake ; 7)
Based on an episode of the television program, Monster by mistake.
ISBN 1-55366-216-4

I. Jarvis, Deborah, 1954- II. CCI Entertainment Ltd. III. Title.
IV. Title: Monster by mistake (Television program) V. Series:
Kropp, Paul, 1948– . Monster by mistake ; 7.

PS8571.R772F68 2002   jC813'.54   C2002-900352-0
PZ7.K93Fo 2002

Winding Stair Press
An imprint of Stewart House Publishing Inc.
290 North Queen Street, #210
Etobicoke, Ontario, M9C 5K4 Canada
1-866-574-6873

Executive Vice President and Publisher: Ken Proctor
Director of Publishing and Product Acquisition: Susan Jasper
Production Manager: Ruth Bradley-St-Cyr
Copy Editing: Martha Campbell
Text Design: Laura Brady
Cover Design: Darrin Laframboise

1 2 3 4 5 6   07 06 05 04 03 02

Printed and bound in Canada

COLLECT THEM ALL

8 BOOKS SO FAR!

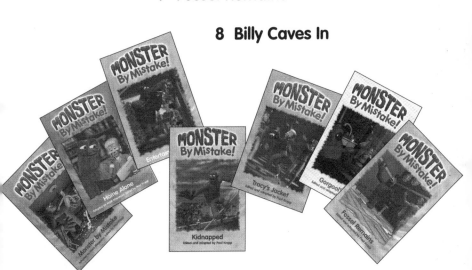

Contents

Chapter 1

The quiet of the Patterson home was broken by the blaring of a trumpet. It was eight-year-old Warren Patterson making the awful noise. He was in his room practicing with Johnny B. Dead, the ghostly friend who lived in their house.

Warren struggled with "The Saints Go Marching In" – his very best song. If only he could get a few more of the notes right.

"Not bad! Not bad at all!" Johnny said, trying to encourage him.

"Soon you'll be another Louis Armstrong?"

"Who?" Warren asked.

"Oh, never mind, kid. Here, the song should go like this." Johnny the Ghost began to play, and then Warren joined in. Together they sounded pretty good.

Warren was making a fine D sharp when his sister Tracy burst into the room.

"Warren," she cried "the Book of Spells is gone! I can't find it anywhere!"

Warren coughed into his trumpet. The cough made a loud *blat*. "Gone?" he asked.

"How can it be gone?" asked Johnny.

"Well," explained Tracy, "I had it out yesterday after school. I was testing a spell that turns vegetables into chocolate. The spell didn't work that well, and I ended up with a lot of soggy brown broccoli—"

"But the book?" Johnny prompted.

"Oh, right," said Tracy. "I was sure I put it back in the chest, like always, but it's not there now!"

"You're sure you looked everywhere?" asked Warren.

"Yes, I'm positive."

Tracy had been very careful to keep the Book of Spells safe. Because of one, silly magic spell, her brother, Warren, turned into a large blue monster every time he sneezed. 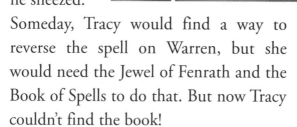 Someday, Tracy would find a way to reverse the spell on Warren, but she would need the Jewel of Fenrath and the Book of Spells to do that. But now Tracy couldn't find the book!

"Tracy, we need it!" Warren exclaimed. "I don't want to turn into the Monster forever. Do you have any idea how embarrassing it would be if anybody found out? How could you just *lose* it?"

"Don't lose your cool, kid," Johnny told Warren. "It's got to be around somewhere. Did you ask your mom?"

"Why would she have it?" replied Tracy.

Warren shook his head in despair. "She's not here anyway. She took a bunch of stuff to the rummage sale at school."

Johnny raised an eyebrow and the two kids looked at each other. "The rummage sale!" they cried in one voice.

Chapter 2

Johnny made himself invisible as he and the kids raced into the schoolyard. Warren and Tracy searched frantically for their mother. It seemed like every family at the school had brought out their junk. At last they found their mom.

"Oh, hi kids!" said Mrs. Patterson, smiling. She was unpacking a cardboard box full of old stuff: toys, clothes and books.

Warren frowned as his mom pulled out some of his old toys. "Hey, that's my model jet! I glued that together all by myself."

"It's for a good cause, sweetie," Mrs. Patterson replied, still unpacking. "The money we raise will buy new playground

equipment. Or maybe some gerbils for the kindergarten class."

Tracy looked over the books on the table and sighed. All she saw were little kids' stories. "Um, Mom? Did you take any books besides these picture books? Anything else?"

"No, nothing else. Well, except some smelly old book on your desk. I threw that in, too."

Tracy was more than a little angry. "I wish you'd asked me first, Mom. Well, not about the picture books, I'm way past that now. But that old book on my desk," Tracy thought fast, "it's a valuable, uh, science book. I need it back!"

Her mother just smiled. "Oh, Tracy. I'm sorry but I just sold it. It's for a good cause, you know."

Warren and Tracy were stunned.

"Who bought it?" stammered Tracy.

"Well, it was some man with white hair. I've never seen him before, but he was very interested in it," she said, tapping her chin thoughtfully. "Oh, there he is over there!" Mrs. Patterson pointed directly behind the two kids.

Turning to look, Warren and Tracy

spotted the man. He wasn't too tall, and wore a simple sweater – no one would look at him twice. But he had the Book of Spells tucked under his arm, and he was leaving the schoolyard!

"Come on!" shouted Tracy. "We've got to get that book back!"

"Bye guys," called Mrs. Patterson.

"Bye Mom!" replied the invisible Johnny.

Mrs. Patterson looked around. "Who said that?" she wondered. With a shrug, she continued unpacking her boxes. How could she have known that Tracy would be so attached to a smelly, old book?

Chapter 3

Tracy and Warren dashed out of the schoolyard to the sidewalk. With Johnny sailing over their heads, they kept just behind the white-haired man. The kids watched him cross the street as a bus pulled up to a stop. Before the kids were able to cross the street, the bus pulled away and the man was gone.

"Oh no!" cried Warren. "He must have gotten on the bus."

"We have to catch it," said Tracy, determined. "And there's only one way, Warren." She looked hard at her brother.

"Okay. If I have to," Warren sighed.

The kids moved off behind some nearby bushes where Tracy pulled off her knapsack and opened it. Quickly, she pulled out a shaker full of pepper and started sprinkling it on Warren's nose. The young boy breathed in deeply. The pepper made him sneeze.

"Ah . . . ah . . . ah-choo!"

With a flash and a sparkle, Warren turned into a very large and very blue monster.

"Let's go," Tracy said.

The Monster took off running after the bus. Tracy and Johnny the Ghost tried to keep up as best they could, but they were no match for the Monster's speed.

The Monster ran faster and faster, slowly gaining on the bus. As he got closer, the Monster reached out and grabbed the rear bumper. He dug in his heels and pulled the bus to a stop.

*   *   *

Inside the bus, Tracy and Warren's father was whistling as he drove along the route. He loved his job as a bus driver. It gave him a chance to relax behind the wheel and enjoy the town of Pickford's scenery. The passengers were friendly and the buses were new. Usually, they worked just fine. So Tom Patterson was amazed when his bus came to a jarring stop.

"What the heck?" he said out loud. He checked the dash lights to see what was going on. That's why he didn't see the Monster climb up the back of the bus and sit on the roof.

Mr. Patterson got off the bus to try to find out what had happened.

Tracy caught up to the bus just as her father stepped out. Luckily, Johnny was still invisible.

"Dad!" cried Tracy, out of breath.

"Tracy?" Mr. Patterson was puzzled.

"Thanks for stopping. I thought I had missed you." Tracy saw the Monster on top of the bus and he gave her a thumbs-up sign. "You can get going again once I get on."

"Hold on a minute. I have to check the brakes," her father said. "This thing came to a funny stop, all by itself."

"Oh, the brakes are fine," said Tracy. She was afraid her dad might look up and see the Monster on top of the bus.

"How do you know?" asked her father.

"Well, after that impressive stop you just made . . ."

"But I never touched the brake pedal!"

"You could've fooled me. Let's go before you get behind schedule. I know how much you hate being late!" said Tracy.

Mr. Patterson smiled at his daughter. "Oh, okay. You have your bus pass? I can't break the rules just because you're my kid."

Tracy just smiled. "I never leave home without it!"

Tracy and her father boarded the bus and Johnny floated up to the Monster's side.

"Way to go, kid," said the ghost.

"Sure is a nice view up here!" said the Monster with a smile.

"Reminds me of a British double decker," Johnny told him.

"Is that some kind of hamburger?" the Monster asked.

Johnny just shook his head as the bus kept rolling.

So far, the kids were doing just fine in their plan to get back the book. But that was before the town bully, a boy named Billy Castleman, saw the Monster on top of the bus.

Chapter 4

Billy Castleman was riding his bike, for once just minding his own business. Billy was famous – or infamous – as the worst bully in the town of Pickford. When he wasn't picking on little kids or kicking garbage cans, he was bugging Warren.

Normally, Billy would not have paid any attention to a town bus. But this particular bus had a large, blue monster on top of it.

"Look at that! It's the Pickford Monster up there!" he shouted.

The Monster spotted Billy and gave him a little wave from his position on top of the bus. The bully looked around and cursed. The street was empty so no one else could see what he did.

Billy pedaled madly, trying to keep up with the bus. The Monster had to laugh at his effort. The bus quickly pulled away, leaving Billy behind.

*   *   *

The bus continued along its route, and still the white-haired man hadn't gotten off. Finally, the bus arrived at the Pickford Museum. The white-haired man got up from his seat and left the bus, carrying the Book of Spells under his arm. Tracy quickly followed him.

As the white-haired man walked towards the museum, Tracy waved at the Monster to get down off the bus. As the bus pulled away, the cloud of exhaust made the Monster sneeze.

"Ah . . . ah . . . ah-choo!"

With a flash and an electric *Fzzzzzip*, the Monster turned into Warren. "Where are we now, Tracy?" asked Warren.

"It's the museum. Let's go. We can't lose that man!"

The kids spotted their target heading to the side of the building with the Book of Spells still under his arm. They took off after him just as Billy Castleman arrived on his bike.

Billy watched Warren and Tracy take off. For quite a while, Billy had suspected that Warren Patterson might really be the Pickford monster. Now he was sure of it!

"He changed back again? How does he do that?" Billy was talking to himself, but he still wanted an answer. If he could show everybody that the Monster was really Warren Patterson, well, that would be so cool! Billy would be famous and Warren might end up in the zoo!

*   *   *

Warren and Tracy watched the grey-haired man approach a door at the side of the building. Taking a security card from his pocket, the man unlocked the door and stepped inside.

As the Patterson kids raced for the door, they heard someone calling behind them.

"Oh, Warren!" shouted Billy in an insulting way. "I mean, oh Monster! I know your secret! I know who you are!"

"Oh no," moaned Warren. "I thought we lost him. How did he get here?"

"We had better get inside," suggested Tracy.

The kids pulled at the now-closed door, but it was locked. Johnny became visible beside the kids and tipped his hat.

"Allow me," he said. Floating straight through the door, Johnny opened it from the inside. That made it easy for the kids to enter the building. But it wasn't going to be easy to get the door closed, as Billy raced up and started pulling on the handle.

"Oh no you don't!" cried Billy, struggling to open the door against Warren. "I saw you on that bus! I know you're the Monster!"

"Prove it!" shouted Warren. With one last heave, the door clicked shut and locked.

Billy tried to open the door, but failed. He cursed his luck as the Patterson kids left him behind.

"You won't get away from me for long!"

he shouted at the closed door. Then the bully ran around to the main doors of the museum.

Chapter 5

Tracy and her brother walked through the halls of the museum with Johnny floating close-by. They had lost sight of the man carrying the Book of Spells, but they knew he had to be somewhere in the building.

"Ah, I love museums," said Johnny. "Do you think we can go check out the dinosaurs?"

"That's got to wait," replied Tracy. "We need to find that man and get the book back."

"Hey, look at this!" Johnny said. The three of them had entered the ancient Egypt display.

"It's just a mummy," Tracy told him.

"My mummy never looked like that," Johnny replied.

"Would you get serious!" Tracy told him. "If we don't get the Book of Spells back, it may be lost forever, and I'll be in big trouble."

As the kids entered a large exhibit hall, they spotted the last person they expected to see.

"Ms. Gish!" said Warren, startled to find his teacher there.

"Well, if it isn't Tracy and Warren," Ms. Gish replied. The old woman was Warren's teacher now and had been Tracy's teacher four years earlier. "It's nice to see you kids here at the museum. There's so much to learn from ancient cultures. I was about to go to the Greek section, and I'd be happy to teach you all about it."

"Thanks, Ms. Gish . . ." stammered Warren, searching for an excuse to get away.

"Warren wants to spend more time looking at the mummies," filled in Tracy.

"Mummies?" asked Ms. Gish. "We covered that quite thoroughly last year, I believe."

Warren gave an embarrassed smile. "What can I say? I like dead things."

Ms. Gish gave him a strange look. She had always thought the Patterson boy was a bit . . . unusual.

"Well, we'll see you later," Tracy declared. The kids dashed off before Ms. Gish could stop them.

Just then, Billy Castleman entered the exhibit room. Ms. Gish spotted him right away and smiled widely. "Are

25

you looking for the ancient Greeks, Billy?"

Billy looked puzzled. "Ancient what?"

"Greeks," she said, grabbing Billy by the arm before he could get away. "I'll guide you. I know all about them!" Despite Billy's protests, she led him directly away from Tracy and Warren.

*   *   *

Meanwhile, the Patterson kids were hopelessly lost. They had been wandering the halls for what felt like ages. There was still no sign of the white-haired man they were trying so hard to catch. They reached yet another fork in the hallways.

"Which way now?" asked Warren.

Tracy looked upset. "I don't know. We've been searching forever and haven't seen a single sign of him."

The kids looked up when they heard a

sharp whistle. Johnny the Ghost floated around a corner and motioned to the kids to follow him. "This way!" he cried. The kids ran to catch up.

Warren and Tracy rounded the corner to find Johnny floating in front of a small office. With a smile he pointed to the closed door. "He's in there," he said proudly.

Tracy thought a moment. "I wonder who he is. He must be important if he has an office in a museum."

Johnny stuck his head in through the door and took a quick look around. "Whoa, that's some office!" exclaimed Johnny when he pulled his head back out.

"What do you mean?" asked Tracy.

"You'll find out," replied Johnny mysteriously.

Warren and Tracy shared a look, and then turned to the door. Warren reached out and knocked. A gruff voice shouted from inside. "Enter!"

The kids jumped. Carefully, Tracy opened the door.

Chapter 6

The door opened into an office that looked as if a tornado had struck. The office had dusty old books lying everywhere. Papers were tossed carelessly over a very large desk. All over the room there were large piles of bones. There were knee bones, arm bones, long bones, short bones and maybe even funny bones lying around the office.

Tracy saw that the grey-haired man had his back to the door. He seemed to be recording some notes into an old tape recorder. "Um, excuse me?" Tracy said.

The man turned to face the Patterson kids.

"Good heavens! Children in my office!" he cried.

Tracy saw that getting her book back

might not be easy. "Actually, we're not children – or only my brother is. I'm almost a teenager," she said proudly. "My name is Tracy, and this is my brother Warren."

"And why have you come barging into my office?" asked the man. "I have important work to do, you know."

"Yes, but, you see . . ." Tracy had just begun when Warren jabbed her in the ribs with his elbow.

"Tracy, look!" he whispered, pointing to the largest skeleton he had ever seen. It was propped in a corner of the office and looked half like a human and half like Tyrannosaurus Rex!

The white-haired man looked quite proud. "Isn't he wonderful, children? That's Pickford Man. He's ten thousand years old and I dug him up myself, right here in Pickford!"

Warren was impressed. "They really let you do that? I mean, dig up bones?"

"My dear boy, I am Dr. Henry Fossel, head of palaeontology here at the museum. I dig up whatever I like," said the man.

"You sure have a lot of bones," noted Tracy.

"They're my life's work. The study of pre-historic man," he sighed, "just isn't

valued. All children want to see these days are mummies and dinosaurs! But what do you children want from me? Why are you here?"

"You have something of ours," said Warren.

"A book," added his sister. "You bought it at a rummage sale this morning."

Dr. Fossell looked at the children with interest. "What do you know about that book?" he asked.

"Er . . . nothing really," said Tracy, trying to cover the truth. "I just want to buy it back from you. My mom really wasn't supposed to sell it at the sale, so I'd like it back now, please."

The old man's eyes narrowed. "Where did you get the book from to begin with?"

"I'm sorry, but. . ." stammered Tracy.

"That's classified information," Warren added cheerfully.

"Oh, I see," replied Dr. Fossel in a

rather insulting tone. "Classified is it? Well, I'm sorry too. I like this old book. I'm going to put it on my coffee table at home. It will go right beside the bones of my sabre-toothed tiger!"

"Dr. Fossel, please," Tracy begged

"The book belongs to me now," he said with a smirk. "Now get out of my office before I call security!"

Frustrated, the children left the office. The door slammed behind them.

"What do we do now?" asked Warren.

"Let me think for a minute," said an irritated Tracy. "We could . . . no."

Warren looked at her.

"Or we could . . . no."

Warren got upset as Tracy kept talking to herself.

"Or maybe we could . . . no."

Then Warren got an idea himself. "I could turn into the Monster! Once he saw me at his door, he'd give the book back, no problem!"

Tracy gave Warren a look that only an older sister can give. "That's dumb, Warren. We don't want to scare him to death."

Just then, Tracy's knapsack began to grow bright blue. The Jewel of Fenrath was inside, powering up for a spell.

"You brought the jewel with you?" asked Warren. "But why?"

"Well, I didn't want to take any chances with Mom selling all of our stuff."

"So why is the jewel glowing?" Warren asked.

Tracy had the answer in a flash. "Dr. Fossel must be using the Book of Spells !"

"You mean he knows how?"

"He must be reading one of the spells!" cried Tracy. "Come on, Warren. We have to stop him before he destroys the whole museum!"

Chapter 7

The kids raced back to Dr. Fossel's door. Frantically, Tracy tried the doorknob, but found it securely locked.

"Johnny!" she called.

Johnny the Ghost appeared in the air. "I'm here."

"Can you look inside and tell us what Dr. Fossel is doing with the book?"

"Sure thing, kid. Hold tight."

Johnny floated above the door and peered through the transom window. He could see Dr. Fossel at his desk, hunched over the book. It looked like he was reading into a microphone connected to an old tape recorder. Johnny dropped back down to give a report.

"He's definitely reading something out of the book," said Johnny.

Tracy was about to speak when her knapsack, now on the floor, glowed even brighter. A bolt of blue lightening shot out from the knapsack. It sped under the door into the office.

*   *   *

Inside the office, Dr. Fossel had just finished his recording. He wanted to get some of the strange words from this mysterious new book onto a tape. It wasn't a language he knew. Not Greek, or Latin or Philadelphian . . . no, but it had a certain rhythm.

Zaaaaap!

Dr. Fossel was startled when blue lightening sped into his office from the hallway.

"What on Earth!" he shouted.

The blue streak hit his desk and bounced off. Then it zoomed directly at the huge skeleton of Pickford Man.

Zooooop!

Striking the skeleton, the bolt disappeared and Dr. Fossel sighed in relief. But his relief turned to horror when the bones jumped down off the stand!

The pile of bones stood up and began looking around. It took one step, then two, then raised its arms. Suddenly Pickford Man was alive!

Dr. Fossel tried to scramble out from behind his desk when the Book of Spells slipped out of his hands. Unfortunately, the book sailed through the air and landed right in the arms of Pickford Man.

The huge skeleton burst through the door of the office. It went right past Warren and Tracy.

"Oh no!" shouted Tracy. "The spell brought that skeleton to life. And it's got the book!"

Johnny the Ghost was startled. "Did I just see what I think I saw?"

Warren dusted himself off and got up. "Pickford Man is on the loose!" he shouted. "Tracy, you help Dr. Fossel. Johnny, you come with me and help get the book back."

The boy and the ghost took off down the hall after Pickford Man.

Tracy picked up her book bag and walked into Dr. Fossel's office. She found the old bone collector and helped him to his feet. "Are you alright?" Tracy asked.

"Yes, I think so," said a very scared Dr. Fossel. "I mean, given that my best exhibit just ran away with the rarest book I've ever seen. Otherwise, I suppose I'm just fine."

Tracy was not sympathetic. "I'm sorry, Dr. Fossel, but it's your own fault. If you had just given me the book then none of this would ever have happened," said Tracy, sternly.

"What are you talking about?"

"You read out loud from the book and activated. . ." Tracy stopped, afraid she had said too much.

"Activated what?"

Tracy put her bag on the cluttered desk and opened it up. She reached inside and pulled out the beautiful Jewel of Fenrath. "This," she said.

"Oh, dear," breathed Dr. Fossel. "How wonderful! Please, may I see it?"

Tracy looked at the old scholar with

mistrust. He had had the Book of Spells for only a few hours, and look what happened. Still, he was a scientist.

"I promise I won't harm it," Dr. Fossel

told her. "I have some knowledge of these types of things."

Dr. Fossel looked so hopeful and sincere that Tracy felt bad for doubting him. "Just be careful with it," she said as she handed him the jewel.

"So this works with that book somehow? It casts. . . magic spells?" asked Dr. Fossel.

"Yes, and I can use it to reverse spells, too. Right now, I've got to reverse the spell that sent Pickford Man running around."

"Of course," said Dr. Fossel as he handed the jewel back to the girl. "I'll do whatever I can to help you."

"You just have to tell me the exact words you said to activate the spell."

Dr. Fossel looked thoughtful. "Well, it was something like *stem ick nematoad. . .* No, that's not right. *Ick stem nebulosity.* No, maybe *ick root stem plantain!*"

"Think, Dr. Fossel," Tracey urged the old scientist.

"Well, there's a bit of a problem, dear." Dr. Fossel admitted. "To tell you the truth, I just don't remember what I said!"

Chapter 8

Warren and Johnny raced through the hallways of the museum as fast as they could manage. They zoomed past ancient tombs, works of art and suits of armour. But Pickford Man seemed to have disappeared.

Warren stopped where two hallways crossed so he could catch his breath. Suddenly the skeleton ran right past him

"There he goes!" cried Warren to Johnny, taking off again.

The large skeleton ran into an exhibit hall full of ancient Greek artifacts. On his way into the room, Warren tripped over a drop-cloth on the floor. In a second, the young Patterson boy fell face first into a pile of plaster dust.

Warren's nose crinkled from the dust

and he couldn't help but let out a sneeze.

Ah . . . ah . . . ah-choo!

With a flash and a sparkle, he trans-
formed into the Monster.

"Now we're talking," said Johnny. "It'll
be easy to tackle Pickford Man with your
monster strength!"

The Monster leapt up and chased after

the running skeleton. But just as Pickford Man came within reach, the Monster heard a voice that stopped him dead in his tracks.

"Here we are, Billy. The Greek displays are in this exhibit hall."

It was Ms. Gish, and she was just about to enter the room. The Monster scrambled to hide behind a nearby pillar, and Johnny faded to invisible.

"Now, let's see how much you've learned, Billy. Who was the first artist to carve marble statues?" Ms. Gish asked as they entered the room.

"Uh, I don't know," said Billy looking miserable. "Maybe Wayne Gretzky."

"Now don't be supercilious, young man. I just told you the name of the artist," she said in frustration. "Look over here. This marble bust is a wonderful example of his work." Ms. Gish walked towards a display of statues.

With the teacher and the bully walking

away from him, the Monster slipped from his hiding place. He was desperate to get out of there before he was discovered. As luck would have it, Billy Castleman chose that moment to turn around.

Billy's eyes widened and his mouth dropped open when he saw the Monster. "I see you, Warren! I know it's you!" shouted Billy, wrenching himself away from Ms. Gish. The Monster bolted out of the room and Billy chased after him. "Come back here!"

Ms. Gish was startled by Billy's sudden escape. She wasn't going to let him get away from her that easily.

"Billy Castleman," she shouted, "come back here!" Ms. Gish took off after her reluctant student just as Pickford Man came back into the hall.

Chapter 9

Back in Dr. Fossel's office, Tracy and the doctor were still working on remembering the spell. Tracy was getting short tempered, and the doctor was so frustrated he was close to pulling his hair out.

"I know there was an "ich" in there somewhere," he said.

"*Ich stem nimoy?*" offered Tracy.

"Yes!" said Dr. Fossel, excited. "Well, maybe. That was part of it. *Nimoy*, now that might not be right. Wasn't he the actor who played Mr. Spock on Star Trek?"

"Dr. Fossel, you have to concentrate!"

"Well, yes, dear. I'm trying. When you get older, you see, the cortex of the brain . . ."

Tracy had had enough. "You keep

thinking, doctor. I'm going to go find my brother." She grabbed the Jewel of Fenrath from his desk and left the office.

*   *   *

An invisible Johnny and the large blue Monster were back wandering through the halls of the museum. Needless to say, They were both getting very tired of this.

"Haven't we passed this statue three times before?" asked the Monster.

"I don't know," replied Johnny. "I think I've lost count." Johnny became invisible again.

The Monster rounded a corner and ran right into something. Too small to be Pickford Man, the Monster looked down to find Billy Castleman looking right back up at him.

"Uh-oh," the Monster said, and ran off. He was trying to escape from Billy just as if he were still Warren's size.

"I've caught you, Warren," taunted the bully, chasing after the Monster. "I'm going to show everybody who you really are! Come back here, you big, blue coward!"

Johnny the Ghost never liked to see his friends getting picked on. This time was no exception. Because he chose not to be seen, Johnny floated down and tripped

Billy. The young bully went sprawling on his face.

"Who did that?" shouted Billy, outraged.

Johnny materialized in front of him. "You have something you want to say to me, kid?"

Billy's jaw dropped open, and then he screamed. Forgetting about the Monster, Billy ran in the opposite direction.

The Monster sighed in relief. "Thanks, Johnny."

"No problem, kid. And look who was calling who a coward! That guy is such a pain!"

A few minutes later, Johnny and the Monster found themselves back in the ancient Greek exhibit room. Realizing that Pickford Man could have returned to the room, the two of them looked around carefully. The room seemed to be empty. From behind him, the Monster heard a voice calling.

"Warren! I'm going to get you!" It was Billy again. He seemed to have forgotten about his fear of the ghost. Now he was going back to his hobby of picking on Warren.

The Monster turned around just as Billy entered the exhibition hall. Thinking quickly, the Monster spotted a small doorway leading to a storage closet. Running over to it, he hid inside.

"It's no use, Warren!" shouted Billy gleefully. "You're trapped now. Your tricks won't scare me away this time!" Doing a happy little dance, Billy strolled towards the cabinet.

Inside the cabinet, all was dark. The Monster couldn't see a thing.

"Johnny, are you here?" asked the Monster.

"Right beside you, kid," came Johnny's reply.

"You can stop holding my hand now."

"But. . . I'm not holding your hand."

"But if it isn't you," wondered the Monster, "then who is it?"

Johnny and the Monster would have looked at each other if the closet wasn't so dark. As it was, they took a moment to think. They reached the same conclusion at the very same second.

"Pickford Man!" they shouted.

Chapter 10

Before Johnny or the Monster could move an inch, Pickford Man burst out of his hiding place. He landed directly in front of the strutting Billy Castleman.

The huge skeleton roared in his face. Billy turned very pale and ran away screaming.

"Yi-yi-yi-yi!"

Warren and Johnny couldn't help but laugh, at least until Pickford Man turned his attention to them.

"Look out!" shouted Johnny.

Pickford Man raised the Book of Spells above his head and tried to hit the Monster with it. The Monster raised his arms up and grabbed hold of the book himself. The two began to struggle.

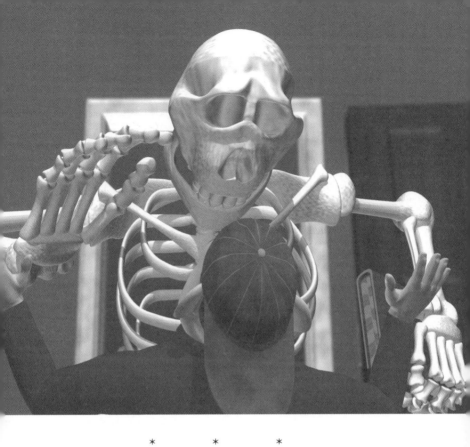

*   *   *

In an office on the other side of the museum, Dr. Fossel paced back and forth, still struggling to remember the words he had spoken earlier.

"*Ich stem niroy ich scap. . .* no! That's not it at all!" he cried in anger.

Defeated, Dr. Fossel kicked his desk. With a clatter, his tape recorder fell to the floor. The white-haired man stared at it for a moment.

"No, could it possibly be?" he said in wonder.

Dr. Fossel grabbed the tape recorder and ran out of the office.

*   *   *

Back in the exhibit hall, Pickford Man struggled with the Monster. Using all of his might, the Monster managed to slip the book out of Pickford Man's hands. That's when Tracy ran into the room.

The Monster spotted his sister and threw the book over to her. "Catch!" he cried.

With no effort, Tracy snagged the Book of Spells out of the air. "Nice toss, Warren! You should play in the Super Bowl."

Tracy's little joke was lost on Pickford

Man, who seemed to have no sense of humor. Even worse, now that Tracy had the book, the skeleton turned towards her.

Tracy backed away, not sure what to do next. "Uhh. . . nice Pickford Man? Wouldn't you rather have some other book?"

Pickford Man said nothing. He continued to advance.

"We could, uh, go to the library and check out some good science fiction for you."

Tracy didn't realize that a 10,000-year-old skeleton probably couldn't read. And he certainly wouldn't enjoy science fiction. All Pickford Man wanted was the Book of Spells. He was almost on top of Tracy when the Monster spoke up.

"Leave her alone!" shouted the Monster. He grabbed Pickford Man's arm and pulled hard on it. He was surprised when the arm came right out of its socket.

"Oh, my, I'm sorry. Really, I am," the Monster cried. He held the arm bones in one hand.

Pickford Man kept coming towards him.

"We can fix this," the Monster said. "We'll get some glue and have you back together in no time. Really, we will."

Pickford Man was not impressed by

the Monster's promises. The giant skeleton was almost on top of him, grinning wickedly.

The Monster stumbled backwards and fell with a thud. "It's just that I don't know my own strength, sometimes. I didn't mean it. I . . . I . . ."

Unfortunately for the Monster, he landed right in the pile of plaster that he'd fallen into before. As a cloud of plaster dust floated around him, the Monster sneezed.

"Ah . . . ah . . . ah-choo!"

And he changed back into Warren Patterson.

The skeleton now had his choice between a trembling 8-year-old Warren, and his not-much-bigger sister Tracy. Which of the children would he attack first?

It was at this very moment that Dr. Fossel burst into the exhibit hall. "*Ich stem nimoy ich scapula tend!*" he shouted.

Tracy quickly pulled the Jewel of Fenrath out of her knapsack. The words Dr. Fossel had just spoken made it glow brightly once more.

"Get back!" cautioned the girl. She aimed the jewel at Pickford Man. Then she shouted the words that would reverse the spell.

"*Bricken blaxen!*"

Chapter 11

After Tracy said the reversing words, a bolt of blue lightning shot from the jewel. It struck Pickford Man with a sizzle.

The skeleton shuddered once, then twice, then slowly fell to the ground. Its bones were scattered everywhere across the floor.

"Nice work, Tracy," Warren told his sister.

"Yes, it was quite impressive," Dr. Fossel agreed.

Dr. Fossel and the Patterson kids carried the bones of Pickford Man into the doctor's office. Both the kids apologized about the skeleton, but Dr. Fossel admitted that all this was his own fault. He said that he'd have Pickford Man put back together in no time. This time, though, he'd glue the bones in place so they wouldn't ever come apart.

"I'm just glad you children weren't hurt," said Dr. Fossel. "I thought I might be too late."

"Well, it was pretty close," Tracy told him. "How did you remember the words to the spell, anyway?"

"I should really have thought of it earlier," Dr. Fossel explained. "When I was reading aloud from your book, I was recording the lines into my tape recorder. Once I remembered that, it was simple. All I did was rewind and play it back."

Tracy and Warren exchanged a look.

"By the way," added Dr. Fossel. "What is this *Bricken blaxen*?"

"It will reverse some spells after you say the original words again," explained Tracy. "Not all spells, I'm afraid, but some."

She looked at her brother. If it were always as simple as *bricken blaxen*, Warren wouldn't have to turn into a monster every time he sneezed.

"Well, I guess you'll want your book back," said Tracy. "You did pay for it." Reluctantly, she held out the book and offered it to the scientist.

Dr. Fossel shook his head. He looked at the book, then up at the determined face of Tracy. "No," he said, "the book

clearly belongs to you. You've earned it."

"Really," she sighed.

"Indeed you have, young lady," Dr. Fossel told her.

Tracy smiled brightly, stowing the book in her bag. "Thank you."

"But perhaps you'd allow me to study the book sometime in the future? I'm very good with ancient languages, so if anything ever puzzles you . . ."

"I'll know exactly where to come," finished the girl. Extending her hand, Dr. Fossel gladly shook it. "Come on, Warren. We had better get home!"

As the kids left Dr. Fossel's office, they saw Billy Castleman with Ms. Gish. He was telling her unbelievable stories.

"So I chased the Monster into a closet, and then this huge skeleton jumped out at me. . ."

Ms. Gish sighed. "Billy Castleman, do you honestly expect me to believe this story?"

"But, he was really big and alive!"

Ms. Gish shook her head and rolled her eyes. "Billy, you're always full of excuses. You'd think you didn't enjoy what I taught you about the ancient Greeks."

"Well, I, uh . . ." for once Billy was at a loss for words.

Ms. Gish saw the Patterson kids coming down the hall of the museum. "Ah, there you are," said Ms. Gish. "Did you children enjoy the museum?"

"It's been very," Tracy paused, "educational."

"We can learn so much from the past," Warren told his teacher. "I'm certain Billy learned even more than we did." Warren looked at the bully and smiled. "Even if no one will ever believe what he says."

Billy had to choke back an angry reply. He watched helplessly as the Patterson kids left the museum and headed home.

The End

Visit the amazing
award-winning
MONSTER
By Mistake!
website

www.monsterbymistake.com

- ❑ experience a 3-D on line adventure
- ❑ preview the next episodes
- ❑ play lots of cool games
- ❑ join the international fan club (it's free)
- ❑ test your knowledge with the trivia quiz
- ❑ visit a full library of audio and video clips
- ❑ enter exciting contests to win GREAT PRIZES
- ❑ surf in English or French

TOP SECRET!

Sneak Preview of New
Monster By Mistake Episodes

Even more all-new monster-iffic episodes of Monster By Mistake are on the way in 2003 and 2004! Here's an inside look at what's ahead for Warren, Tracy and Johnny:

- It promises to be a battle royale when a superstar wrestler comes to town and challenges the Monster to a match at the Pickford arena.

- There's a gorilla on the loose in Pickford, but where did it come from? It's up to the Monster, Tracy and Johnny to catch the gorilla and solve the mystery.

- When making deliveries for a bakery, Warren discovers who robbed the Pickford Savings and Loan. Can the Monster stop the robbers from getting away?

- Warren, Tracy and Johnny visit Fenrath, the home to Gorgool, the Book of Spells and the jewel. In Fenrath, they discover who imprisoned Gorgool in the ball and what they must do to restore order to this magical kingdom.

MONSTER By Mistake! Videos

Six Monster By Mistake home videos are
available and more are on the way.

Each video contains 2 episodes and comes with a special Monster surprise!

Only $9.99 each.

Monster By Mistake & Entertaining Orville
1-55366-130-3

Fossel Remains & Kidnapped 1-55366-131-1

Monster a Go-Go & Home Alone 1-55366-132-X

Billy Caves In & Tracy's Jacket 1-55366-202-4

Campsite Creeper & Johnny's Reunion
1-55366-201-6

Gorgool's Pet & Jungle Land
1-55366-200-8

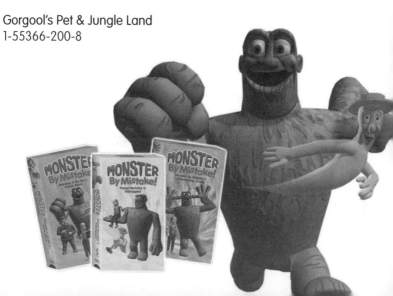

About the people who
brought you this book

Located in Toronto, Canada, **CCI Entertainment** has been producing quality family entertainment since 1982. Some of their best known shows are "Sharon Lois and Bram's The Elephant Show," "Eric's World," and of course, "Monster By Mistake"!

Catapult Productions in Toronto wants to entertain the whole world with computer animation. Now that we've entertained you, there are only 5 billion people to go!

Mark Mayerson grew up loving animated cartoons and now has a job making them. "Monster By Mistake" is the first TV show he created.

Paul Kropp is an author, editor and educator. His work includes young adult novels, novels for reluctant readers, and the bestselling *How to Make Your Child a Reader for Life*.